Dedicated to those who keep me
from completely unraveling.

————————

NANCY PAULSEN BOOKS
Published by the Penguin Group
Penguin Group (USA) LLC
375 Hudson Street, New York, NY 10014

USA | Canada | UK | Ireland | Australia
New Zealand | India | South Africa | China
penguin.com
A Penguin Random House Company

Library of Congress Cataloging-in-Publication Data is available upon request.

Manufactured in China by South China Printing Co. Ltd.
ISBN 978-0-399-16914-4
1 3 5 7 9 10 8 6 4 2

Design by Ryan Thomann. Text set in Estilo Text.
The art for this book was made first with pencils and then with pixels.

Edmund UNRAVELS

words and pictures by
Andrew Kolb

NANCY PAULSEN BOOKS ✺ AN IMPRINT OF PENGUIN GROUP (USA)

It's funny—when talking about a ball of yarn, the end is actually the beginning.

This end, for example . . .

is the beginning of Edmund Loom.

A little ball of energy, he was always

on the lookout for adventure.

From the time he could roll,
Edmund loved to bounce down
the three stairs to explore.

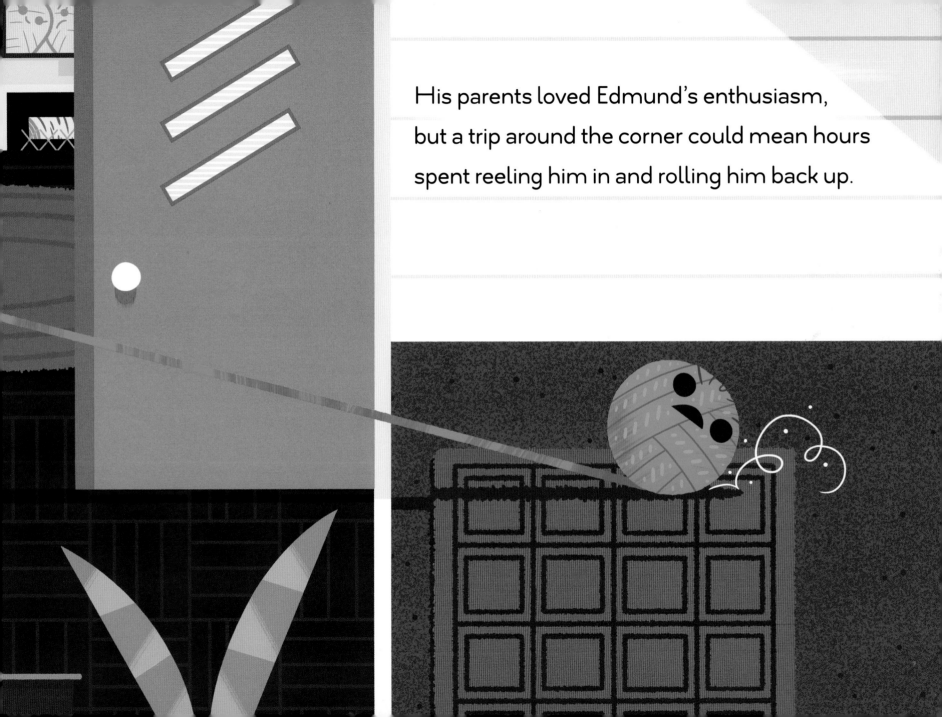

His parents loved Edmund's enthusiasm,
but a trip around the corner could mean hours
spent reeling him in and rolling him back up.

Edmund tried his best to keep it together.
On most days, he kept to a routine of breakfast,
school, chores, dinner, and then finally bed.

But some days Edmund just couldn't resist the tug of discovery.

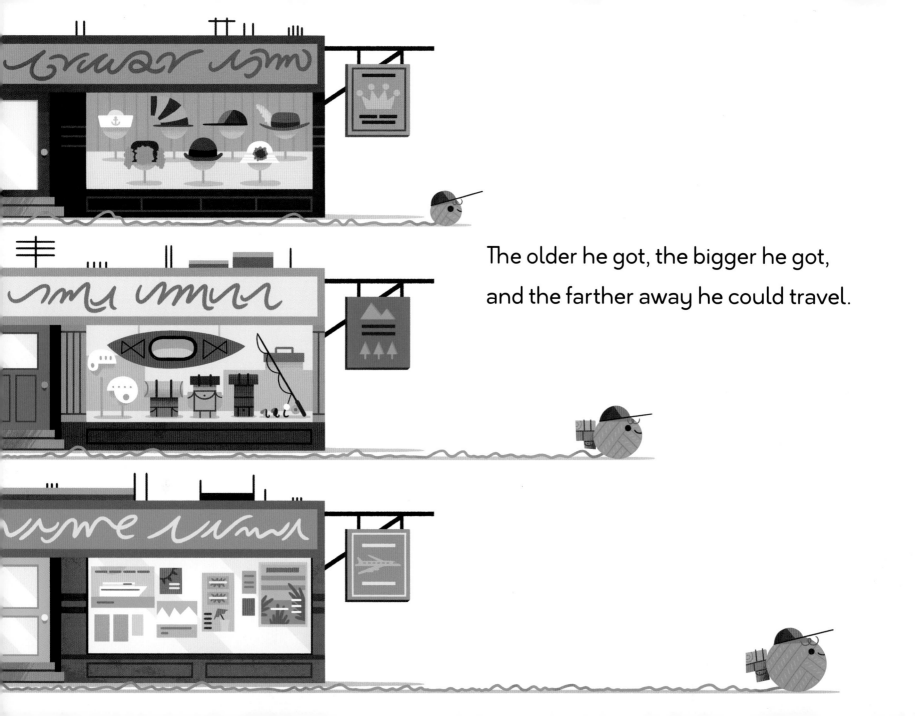

The older he got, the bigger he got,
and the farther away he could travel.

His parents found it harder
and harder to pull him back.

Edmund loved the sights and the sounds of new places.

He was having so much fun he thought
he might never go back home.

There were challenges and scary times too,
but even those were part of the adventure.

There was so much
to experience.

And so many interesting people to meet.

If his parents could see what he was up to,
they would be so surprised!

Soon Edmund realized how far he was from home and that something was missing.

Edmund felt sad and alone.

The sights and sounds
just weren't as much fun.

Then Edmund noticed a welcome
tug—and the joy of bouncing up
three very familiar stairs!

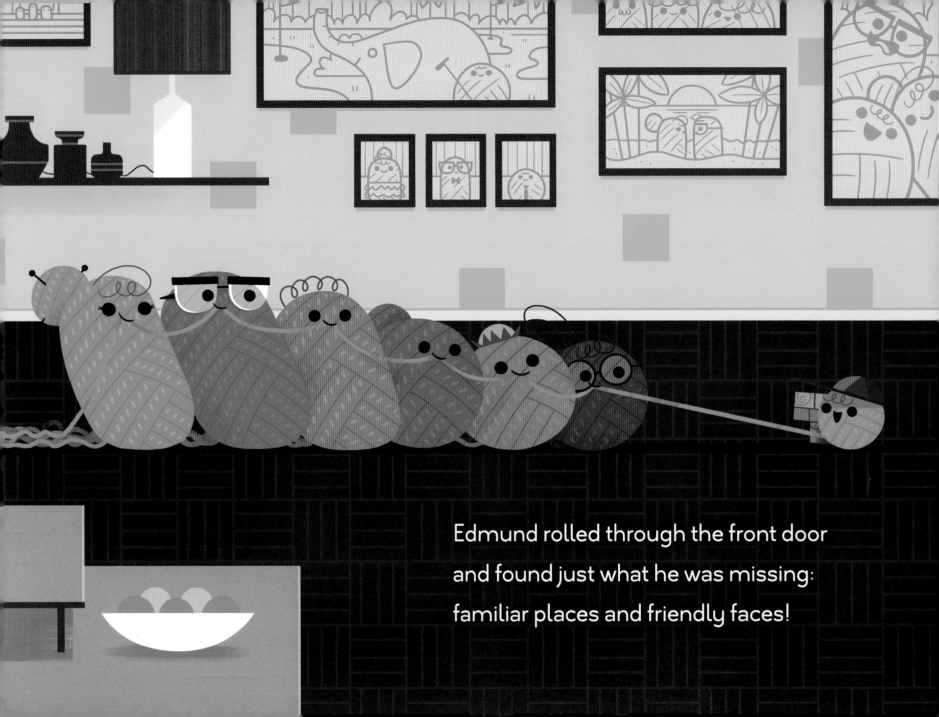

Edmund rolled through the front door
and found just what he was missing:
familiar places and friendly faces!

His family and friends had all pulled together to bring Edmund home and roll him back up.

Of course Edmund continued to journey, but now he was sure to visit home before completely unraveling.

Besides, when there's nothing left but the beginning of a ball of yarn, it's actually . . .

the end.

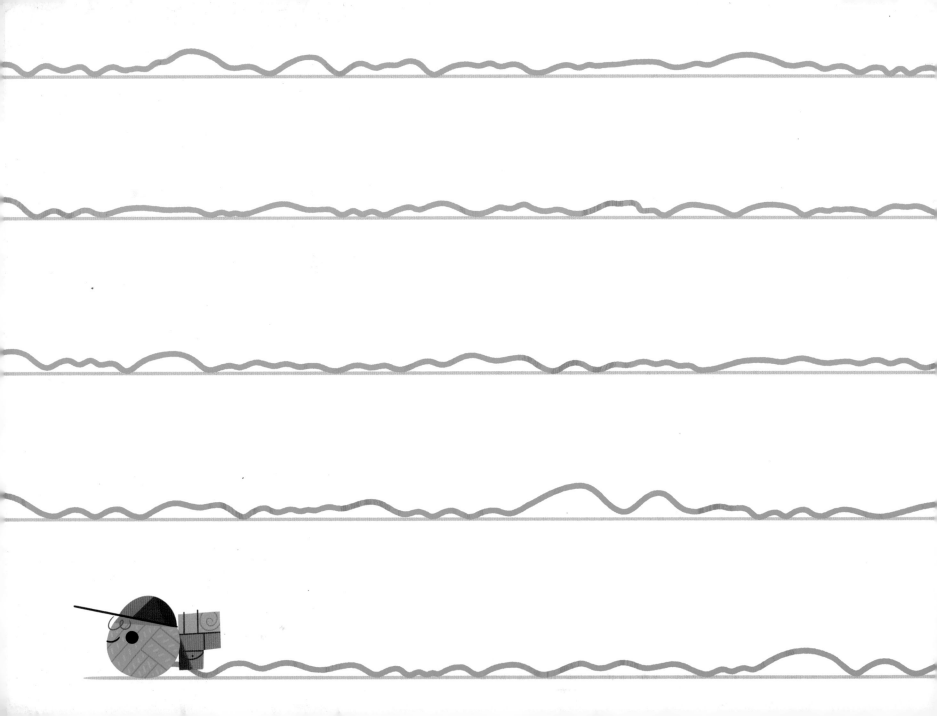